D0486662

This
Frog book
belongs to:

....

This paperback edition first published in 2014 by Andersen Press Ltd.
20 Vauxhall Bridge Road, London SW1V 2SA.
First published in Great Britain in 2003 by Andersen Press Ltd.
Published in Australia by Random House Australia Pty.,
20 Alfred Street, Milsons Point, Sydney, NSW 2061.

Colour separated in Switzerland by Photolitho AG, Zürich.
Printed and bound in China by Foshan Zhaorong Printing Co., Ltd.

10 9 8 7 6 5 4 3 2 1

British Library Cataloguing in Publication Data available.
ISBN 978 1 78344 152 5

Frog
is Sad

Max Velthuijs

Andersen Press

Frog woke up feeling sad . . .

. . . he felt like crying, but he didn't know why.

Little Bear was worried. He wanted Frog
to be happy.
"Please smile, Frog," he said.
"I can't," said Frog.
"But you could *yesterday*," said Little Bear.

But Frog couldn't smile today.
And he couldn't be happy.
And he wanted to be on his own.
So Little Bear went away.

Rat came by. “Cheer up, Frog!” he said.
“I can’t,” said Frog.
“But it’s such a beautiful day!” said Rat. “You’re not sick, are you?”
“No,” said Frog. “I’m not sick. I’m just sad.”

“Shall I make you laugh?” said Rat.
And he began to dance madly about.
But it didn’t make Frog laugh.

Then, Rat walked on his hands . . .
but it didn't cheer Frog up.

Then he balanced a ball on his nose,
just like in the circus!

Frog didn't even smile.

Rat was disappointed. He didn't know what else to do.
And then he had an idea . . .

He rushed off to fetch his violin . . . .

. . . and he started to play a beautiful tune, a tune so beautiful that Frog began to cry. He cried until the tears streamed down his cheeks.

And the more Rat played his violin, the harder Frog cried.
"But Frog, why are you crying?" asked Rat.
"Because you play so beautifully," wept Frog.
He was overcome with emotion.

At that, Rat burst out laughing.
"Oh, you are *silly*, Frog," he said.
He laughed and laughed.
Frog just stood there . . .

Then, suddenly, he began to smile.
His smile grew and grew . . .

. . . until he was laughing and singing and
dancing with Rat, all his sadness gone.

They made such a happy noise
that Duck came running . . .

. . . and Pig and Hare . . .

. . . and Little Bear last of all.
They all fell about, roaring with laughter together.

“Oh!” gasped Frog. “I have never laughed so much in my whole life, ever!”

“Dear Frog,” said Little Bear. “I’m so glad you can smile again. But why were you so sad in the first place?”

“I don’t know,” said Frog. “I just was.”

Max Velthuijs's twelve beautiful stories about **Frog** and his friends first started to appear twenty five years ago and are now available as paperbacks, e-books and apps.

Frog is a Hero
Max Velthuijs
9781783441440
Frog and the Birdsong
Max Velthuijs
9781783441532
Frog Finds a Friend
Max Velthuijs
9781783441501
Max Velthuijs
Frog is Frightened
9781783441426
Frog in Winter
Max Velthuijs
9781783441471
Frog in Love
Max Velthuijs
9781783441457
Frog is Sad
Max Velthuijs
9781783441525
Frog and the Stranger
Max Velthuijs
97811783441433
Frog and the Treasure
Max Velthuijs
9781783441518
Frog and a Very Special Day
Max Velthuijs
9781783441495
Frog and the Wide World
Max Velthuijs
9781783441488
Frog is Frog
Max Velthuijs
9781783441419

Max Velthuijs (Dutch for Field House) lived in the Netherlands, and received the prestigious Hans Christian Andersen Medal for Illustration. His charming stories capture childhood experiences while offering life lessons to children as young as three, and have been translated into more than forty languages.

'Frog is an inspired creation – a masterpiece of graphic simplicity.'
GUARDIAN

'Miniature morality plays for our age.' IBBY